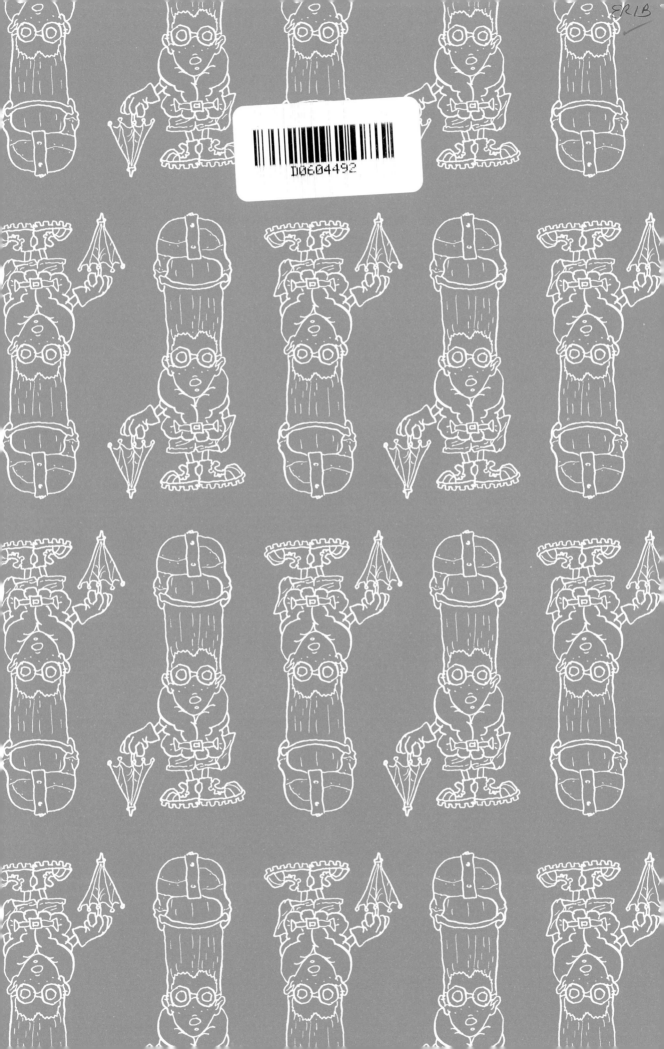

~~ THE ~~
UNEXPECTEDLY
BAD HAIR
OF BARCELONA SMITH

BY

KEITH
GRAVES

PHILOMEL
BOOKS

PHILOMEL BOOKS A division of Penguin Young Readers Group.
Published by The Penguin Group. Penguin Group (USA) Inc., 375 Hudson Street,
New York, NY 10014, U.S.A. Penguin Group (Canada), 90 Eglinton
Avenue East, Suite 700, Toronto, Ontario, Canada M4P 2Y3
(a division of Pearson Penguin Canada Inc.) Penguin Books
Ltd, 80 Strand, London WC2R 0RL, England. Penguin
Ireland, 25 St. Stephen's Green, Dublin 2, Ireland (a
division of Penguin Books Ltd.) Penguin Group
(Australia), 250 Camberwell Road, Camberwell, Victoria
3124, Australia (a division of Pearson Australia Group
Pty Ltd). Penguin Books India Pvt Ltd, 11 Community
Centre, Panchsheel Park, New Delhi - 110 017, India.
Penguin Group (NZ), Cnr Airborne and Rosedale
Roads, Albany, Auckland 1310, New Zealand (a
division of Pearson New Zealand Ltd). Penguin
Books (South Africa) (Pty) Ltd, 24 Sturdee Avenue,
Rosebank, Johannesburg 2196, South Africa. Penguin
Books Ltd, Registered Offices: 80 Strand, London
WC2R 0RL, England.

Published simultaneously in Canada. Manufactured
in China by South China Printing Co. Ltd. Design by Gina
DiMassi. Text set in Kane. The illustrations are rendered in
acrylic on illustration board. Library of Congress Cataloging-
in-Publication Data Graves, Keith. The unexpectedly bad hair of
Barcelona Smith / Keith Graves. p. cm. Summary: Barcelona Smith
is too cautious to even smile for fear of getting a bug in his teeth, until
the day his usually perfectly coiffed locks rebel and teach him to let his
hair down. [1. Hair—Fiction. 2. Play—Fiction.] I. Title. PZ7.G77524Umx
2006 [E]—dc22 2005025047 ISBN 0-399-24273-2 10 9 8 7 6 5 4 3 2 1
First Impression

He never stopped to smell the roses.
It was far too dangerous. Roses were
thorny things and could draw blood.
So Barcelona steered clear.

Barcelona Smith was properly prudent.

For Nancy.

—K. G.

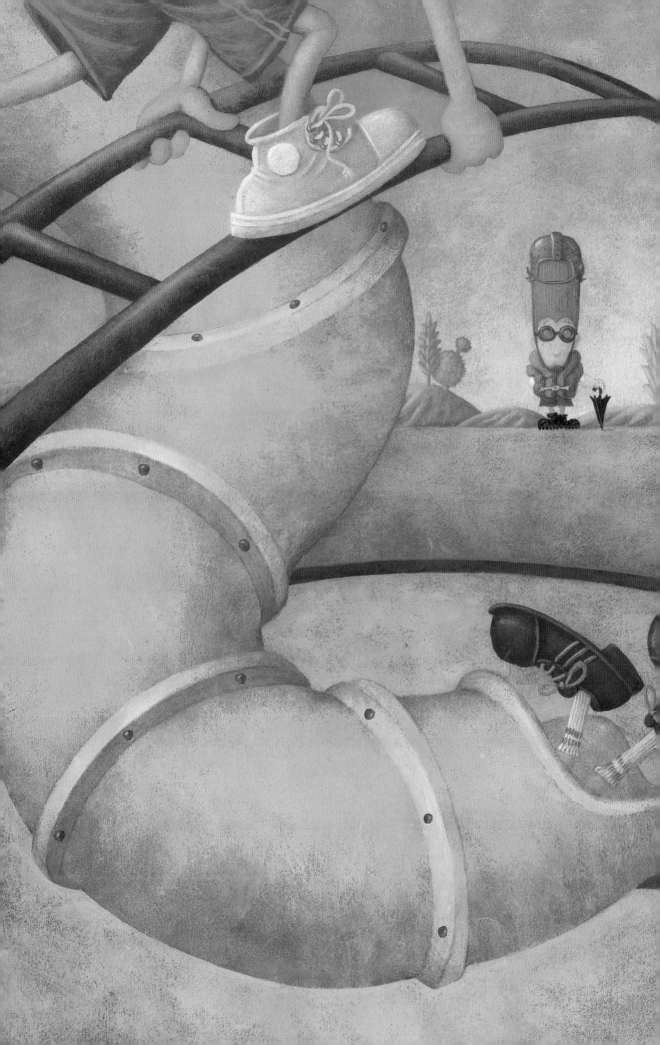

Barcelona Smith avoided
playgrounds altogether. Swings were
most untrustworthy contraptions. Who
knew what injuries might occur on the slide?
And of course, we needn't even speak of the
monkey bars!

Barcelona Smith stayed away
from pets. After all, they were
animals. Animals were known to
be germy and sometimes slobbery.
He might catch a disease. He simply
could not risk it.

And Barcelona Smith never smiled.
The pitfalls of smiling were obvious.
What if a flying insect were to crash
into one's exposed teeth? The thought
of it made Barcelona shudder. As a
result of all his practical prudence,
nothing accidental ever happened to
Barcelona Smith. In fact, nothing at
all ever happened to him.

Then one humid Wednesday,
Barcelona's hair ran amuck.
His hair had always been
well-disciplined before. Clean,
orderly, and exceedingly stiff.
It was predictably prudent hair.

But on this day, the Smith hair
went bananas. The strands uncoiled,
the curls unkinked, the coif unstuck.
Every follicle fooped.

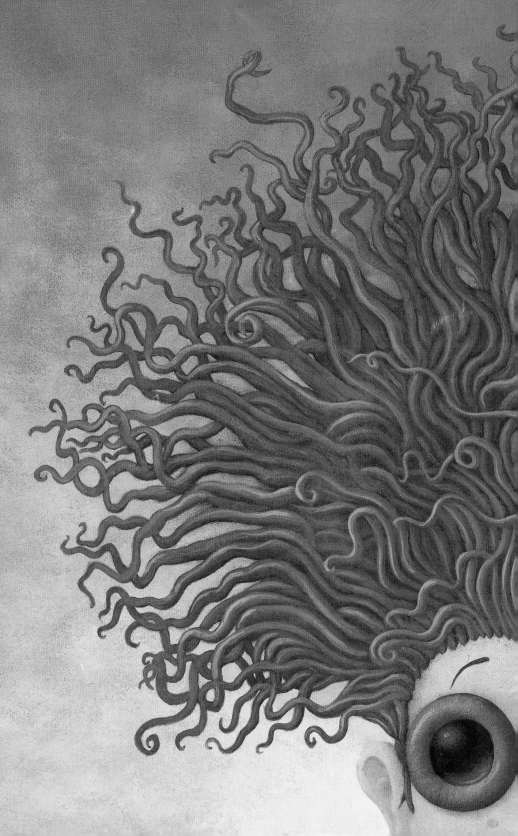

At great risk of injury, Barcelona Smith's hair danced across the room. Barcelona had no choice but to follow. Out the front door and into the yard they went, with no umbrella despite a threatening cloud.

His hair skated down the sidewalk, climbed up a tree, jumped over a rope, stomped through a puddle, and rode a bike. All with daredevil abandon. Barcelona Smith was out of control.

He considered his options. He'd already
tried fretting with all his might, but that
had changed nothing. The prudent choice,
strangely, appeared to be to simply accept
that he was out of control. So Barcelona
Smith allowed himself to gasp. "Eeek."
It felt great, as though he had eaten
a warm apple muffin.

On they went.

Puppies were petted.

Roses were sniffed.

Monkey bars were monkeyed upon.

Evening arrived quite unexpectedly.
Barcelona had been scraped and pricked
and scratched and slobbered on. Every
event that he'd been prudently preventing
had happened that day. Well, almost
every event . . .

That's when it rained. Barcelona's
hair became limp and drippy, soaking
up each drop thirstily. Barcelona
did the same.

At that moment Barcelona Smith
did the most imprudent thing of all.
He smiled. It was a reckless thing to do,
he knew, but he felt the risk just might
be worth it.

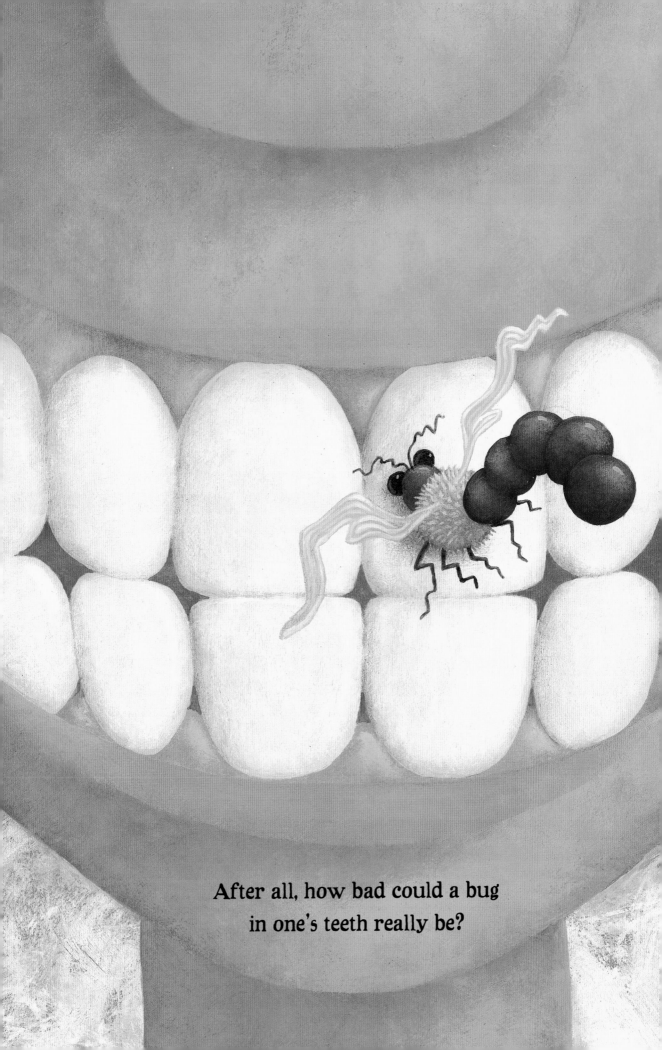

After all, how bad could a bug
in one's teeth really be?